# SHEROES

# JOAN of ARC

Calico Kid
An Imprint of Magic Wagon
abdobooks.com

by **CHRISTINE PLATT**
illustrated by **ADDY RIVERA**

**Christine A. Platt** is an author and scholar of African and African-American history. A beloved storyteller of the African diaspora, Christine enjoys writing historical fiction and non-fiction for people of all ages. You can learn more about her and her work at christineaplatt.com.

*For Madhuri Pavamani. Love you!* —CP

*To those who work to make our world a better place.* —AR

abdobooks.com

Published by Magic Wagon, a division of ABDO, PO Box 398166, Minneapolis, Minnesota 55439. Copyright © 2020 by Abdo Consulting Group, Inc. International copyrights reserved in all countries. No part of this book may be reproduced in any form without written permission from the publisher. Calico Kid™ is a trademark and logo of Magic Wagon.

Printed in the United States of America, North Mankato, Minnesota.
092019
012020

Written by Christine Platt
Illustrated by Addy Rivera
Edited by Bridget O'Brien
Art Directed by Candice Keimig

Library of Congress Control Number: 2019942285

Publisher's Cataloging-in-Publication Data

Names: Platt, Christine, author. | Rivera, Addy, illustrator.
Title: Joan of Arc / by Christine Platt ; illustrated by Addy Rivera.
Description: Minneapolis, Minnesota : Magic Wagon, 2020. | Series: Sheroes
Summary: This title introduces readers to Joan of Arc and how she became a shero to help deliver France from English domination.
Identifiers: ISBN 9781532136436 (lib. bdg.) | ISBN 9781644943090 (pbk.) | ISBN 9781532137037 (ebook) | ISBN 9781532137334 (Read-to-Me ebook)
Subjects: LCSH: Joan of Arc, Saint, 1412-1431--Juvenile literature. | France--Juvenile literature. | Christian women saints--France--Biography--Juvenile literature. | France--History--Charles VII, 1422-1461--Juvenile literature. | Women soldiers--Juvenile literature.
Classification: DDC 944.026 [B]--dc23

# Table of Contents

# CHAPTER 1

# Girl with a Dream

In 1412, Jacques d'Arc and Isabelle Romée welcomed a daughter. They named her Jeanne.

The peasants lived in the village of Domrémy in northeastern France. Little did they know she would become France's shero, Joan of Arc.

In the 1400s, part of France was under English rule. This was during the Hundred Years' War. Joan's family was loyal to France.

Their village was surrounded by English lands. It was often attacked. Once, the English set fire to several properties. They nearly burned Joan's village to the ground.

Joan's family went to church regularly. But she didn't know how to read and write. This didn't stop her from dreaming.

She dreamed of France being free of England's control. Joan longed for her village to live in peace.

Joan loved spending time in her father's garden. She had her first vision there when she was around twelve years old.

In her vision, she saw three archangels appear. They gave her a message that matched her dreams. God had chosen her to help France gain its freedom.

Joan thought they were so beautiful that she cried.

When she was almost a young woman, Joan began her mission. She would follow God's plans for her life. She would free France from English rule.

# CHAPTER #2
## Woman on a Mission

France's troubles with England began in 1420. France's King Charles VI had signed a treaty. It said his daughter must marry England's King Henry V. After the marriage, Henry was the ruler of both countries.

In 1422, Charles VI and Henry V died. Henry VI became the next ruler. England started to occupy northern France. This included Joan's village.

ENGLAND

English Channel

• Reims

☆ Paris

DOMRÉMY
○

Atlantic
Ocean

FRANCE

ENGLISH
Occupied

FRENCH
Occupied

Joan had more visions. One showed the only way the English would leave France. Charles VI's son, Charles VII, had to become king.

This seemed like an impossible feat for a woman. But it became Joan's purpose.

Joan faced many challenges. The first came when she was sixteen. Her father arranged for her to marry. She refused.

She went to the local court. She argued that she should not be forced to marry. She won!

Soon after, Joan started on her plan to meet with Charles VII. She met many people along the way. They were convinced that God had sent her to save France. They began to follow and support her.

Some did not believe a woman could save France. Others thought she needed official permission to meet with the king.

Joan did not give up. She did something that was unthinkable. She cut off her hair and dressed like a man. Then she began a long journey through enemy territory to find Charles.

## CHAPTER #3
# So Smart, So Brave

In the 1400s, men had more rights than women. They were more respected too. Joan was smart to dress like a man. She could travel freely.

Joan's decision was also brave. If she was discovered, she would have faced serious punishment and possibly death.

Joan's disguise worked. She finally met with Charles. Joan made him a promise.

If he allowed her to be his guide, she would lead him to the city of Reims. She would overthrow the English. She would make sure he became king of France.

Charles had many counselors and generals. All of them were men.

They did not think Joan could carry out such a bold promise because she was a woman. They wanted her to prove she had a connection with God.

Every question that was asked of her, Joan answered correctly. Charles was convinced. God had sent Joan to help him get the throne. He gave her an army.

In March 1429, Joan and her army were ready for their first battle. Joan dressed in white armor and also rode a white horse. She led her troops into battle in the French city of Orléans.

The battle was dangerous. But Joan and her army won. The English were forced to flee.

Joan's victory was celebrated across France. She was given the honorable nickname, Maid of Orléans.

For several months after, Joan and her army fought in many battles. They made their way toward the city of Reims.

In July 1429, Joan delivered on her promise. Charles was crowned King Charles VII of France.

# CHAPTER #4
# A Real Shero

Joan seemed destined for greatness after her victory. But some people were jealous of her success and popularity.

Soon, leaders feared that Joan had too much power. They were especially worried because she was a woman.

Joan dealt with jealousy from her homeland. England also wanted to get back at her for winning Orléans.

In the spring of 1430, Joan was captured by English allies. Authorities sentenced her to trial.

Joan was charged with breaking dozens of laws. One of them was for dressing like a man. Others were meant to discourage her followers.

For example, Joan was accused of being a witch. People were superstitious at this time. No one wanted to be a friend or follower of a witch.

King Charles VII was one of them. Even after everything Joan had done, he refused to help her.

Joan was in prison for a year. In May 1431, English authorities gave her a final demand. She could confess that she lied about her mission. Or she would be sentenced to death.

Joan wanted to be freed from jail. She said that she'd never had visions or received messages from God.

But the authorities sent Joan
back to her cell. Days later, she
was charged for dressing like a man
again. This time, the court sentenced
her to death.

Joan was executed on May 30, 1431. She was burned at the stake. This punishment was common for women who were thought to be witches. Joan was nineteen years old when she died.

Joan's legacy did not die with her. Her name continued to rise in fame and popularity. This was because of her loyalty and faithfulness to France.

Even to this day, Joan of Arc is considered a historical shero. She is one of the Roman Catholic Church's most beloved saints.